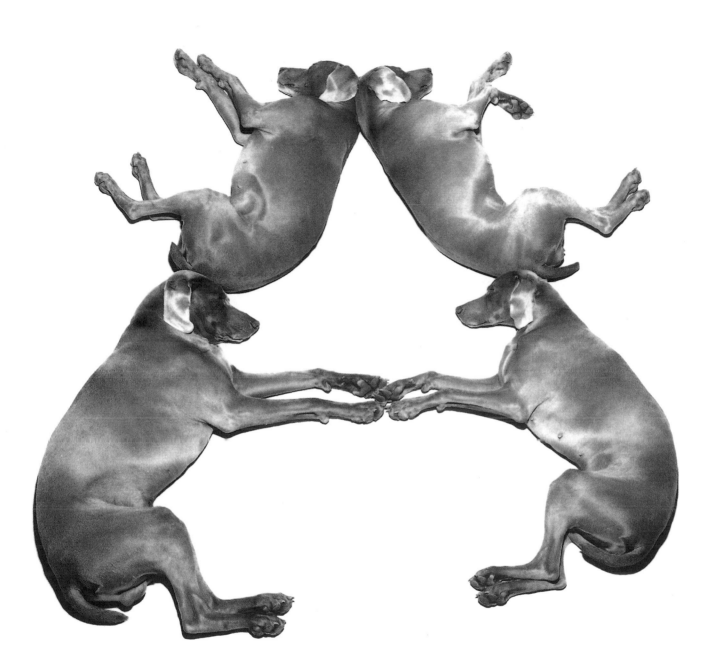

William Wegman

HYPERION
NEW YORK

To Christine

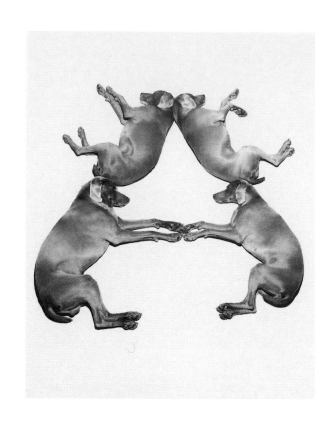

Batty can't

But Batty can balance a

on her head. Can you?

Chundo is standing on a

Careful!

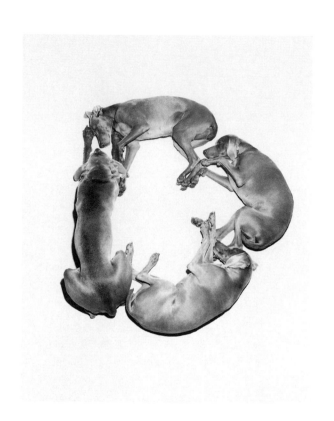

Many of Fay's friends are

Batty has a sock on her nose.

She thinks she looks like an

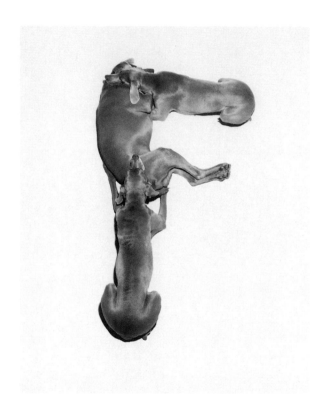

Batty and Fay are

They make a pretty picture.

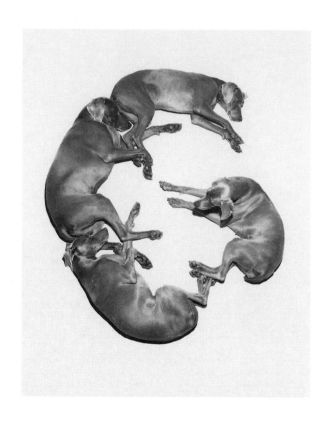

Fay is glamorous in her gorgeous gloves and

Isn't Fay great!

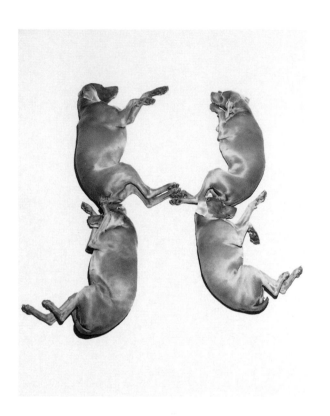

Hi,

Hello, Fay!

Ironically, Batty finds

interesting.

Batty's a

What a joker! Care to join her?

A kiss is just a

What is this?

Fay and Batty are lying under a

Are they lying? Are they lazy?

Who's afraid of a scary

Fay is caught in a

Was she naughty? Not really.

"Pawden me," says Fay to Batty. "Your

is on me. Pawden me."

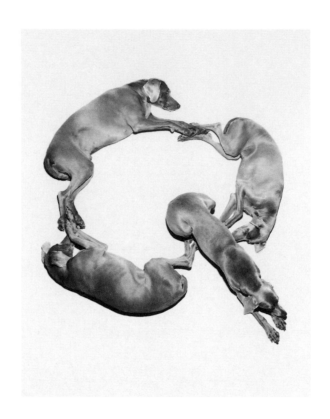

The

felt queasy so she quit.

The rooster is really

but is it really a rooster?

Fay is no flake. She caught a

For heaven's sake, what is Fay
doing with a snowflake?

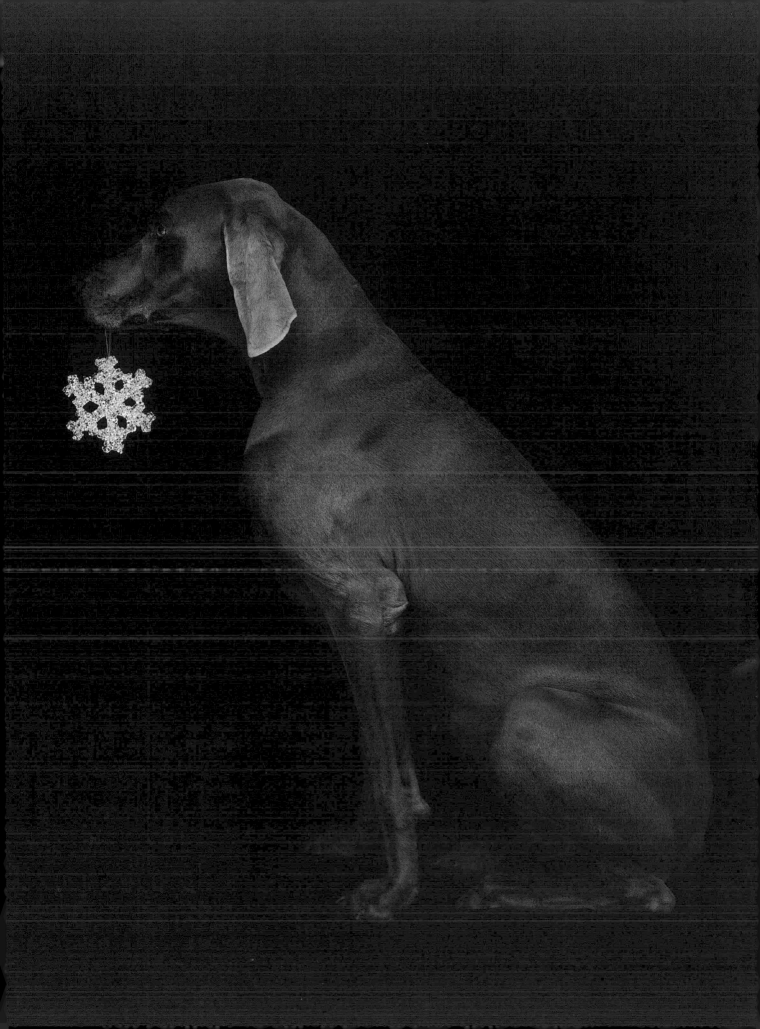

Fay has a

but is it Fay's tail?

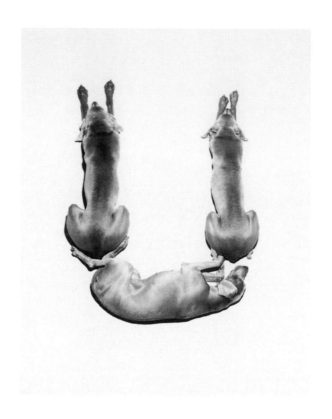

Batty is

Fay, or is it Fay who is under Batty?

Who will be Batty's

Well, who is

whom?

Let's

Fay Ray.

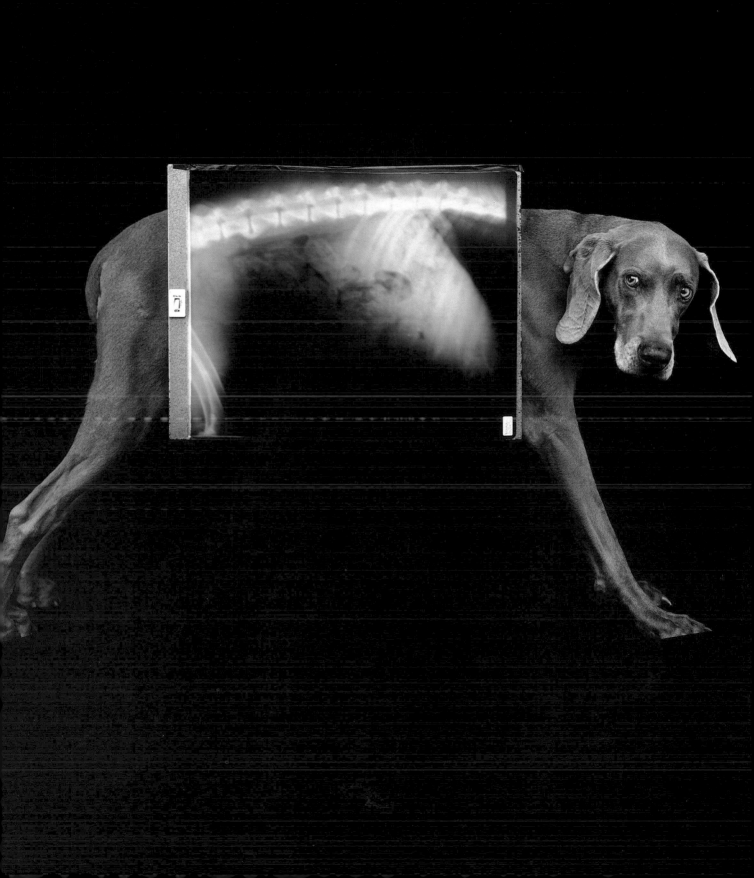

Y is for the color

Does anybody know why?

Can this be a

zoologically speaking?
Fay and Batty think so.

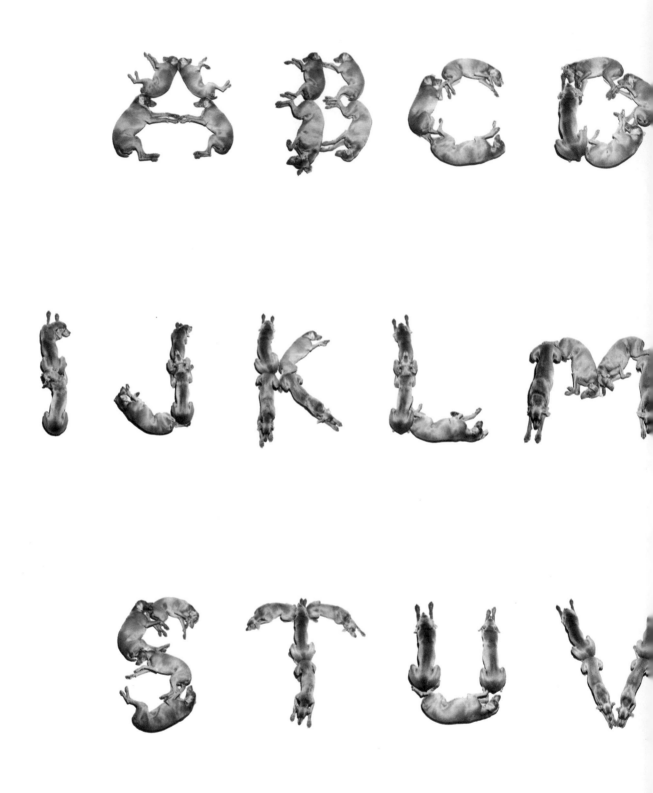

TEXT, PHOTOGRAPHS, AND ALPHABET

For information address
Hyperion Books for Children,
114 Fifth Avenue, New York, New York 10011.
First Edition
3 5 7 9 10 8 6 4 2
Library of Congress Cataloging-in-Publication Data
Wegman, William.
ABC/William Wegman.
p. cm.
ISBN 1-56282-696-4 (trade)—ISBN 1-56282-699-9 (lib. bdg.)
1. English language—Alphabet—Juvenile literature.
2. Weimaraners (Dogs)—Pictorial works—Juvenile literature.
3. Photography of dogs—Juvenile literature. [1. Alphabet. 2. Dogs.] I. Title.
PE1155.W35 1994
421'.1[E]—dc20
93-33637   CIP   AC

DESIGN: DRENTTEL DOYLE PARTNERS
This book is set in 24-point Cloister and 60-point Weimaraner.

ACKNOWLEDGMENTS
WITH THANKS TO
Andrea Beeman, Jason Burch, Christine Burgin, Andrea Cascardi,
Drenttel Doyle Partners, Stacy Fischer, Eric Jeffreys,
Dave McMillan, The Pace/MacGill Gallery, John Reuter, John Slyce,
Katleen Sterck, and Pam Wegman.

WEIMARANERS
Letters: Fay Ray, Battina, Chundo, and Crooky
Color Polaroids: Fay Ray, Battina, Chundo, Crooky, and Laredo

All black-and-white photographs were taken with a Polaroid
Land pack camera using Polaroid Type 665 film. All color pictures were
taken with a Polaroid 20-by-24-inch camera.